The Hungry Thing

by Jan Slepian and Ann Seidler

pictures by Richard E. Martin

ISBN 0-590-42292-8

12 11 10 9 8 7   2 3/9

One morning a Hungry Thing came to town. He sat on his tail. He pointed to a sign around his neck that said Feed Me. The townspeople gathered around to see the Hungry Thing.

"What would you like to eat?" asked the townspeople.

"Shmancakes," answered the Hungry Thing.

"Shmancakes!" cried the townspeople. "How do you eat them? What can they be?"

"Why, dear me," said a Wiseman, "Shmancakes,
that's plain,
   Are a small kind of chicken that falls with the rain."

"Of course," said a Cook, "shmancakes, I've read,
Are better to eat when you stand on your head."

"I think," said a little boy, "you're all very silly.
Shmancakes . . . sound like
Fancakes . . . sound like . . .

Pancakes to me."

So the townspeople gave the Hungry Thing some.

The Hungry Thing ate them all up. Then the Hungry Thing pointed to his sign that said Feed Me.

"What would you like to eat?" asked the townspeople.

"Tickles," answered the Hungry Thing.

"Tickles!" cried the townspeople. "How do you eat them? What can they be?"

"Why, dear me," said the Wiseman, "tickles, you know, Are curly tailed hot dogs that grow in a row."

"Of course," said the Cook, "tickles taste yummy,
And you giggle and laugh with ten in your tummy!"

"I think," said the little boy, "it's all very clear.
Tickles . . . sound like
Sickels . . . sound like . . .

Pickles to me."
And they gave the Hungry Thing some.
The Hungry Thing ate them all up.

"He's underfed.
Have some bread,"
Said a lady
Dressed in red.

"It seems to me
He'd like some tea,"
Said a fellow
Up a tree.

"A bit of rice
Might be nice,"
Said a baby,
Sucking ice.

The Hungry Thing just shook his head and pointed to his sign that said Feed Me.

The townspeople tried again. "What would you like to eat?" asked the townspeople.

"Feetloaf," answered the Hungry Thing.

"Feetloaf!" cried the townspeople. "How do you eat it? What can it be?"

"Why, dear me," said the Wiseman, "feetloaf . . .
let's see . . .
It's a kind of shoe pudding that grows in a tree."
"Of course," said the Cook, "feetloaf tastes sweet,
And it's eaten by kings when they dine in bare feet."

"I think," said the little boy, "you all ought to know.
Feetloaf . . . sounds like
Beetloaf . . . sounds like . . .

Meatloaf to me.''

So the townspeople gave the Hungry Thing some.

The Hungry Thing ate it all up. He again pointed to his
sign that said Feed Me.

''What would you like to eat this time?''
asked the townspeople.

''Hookies,'' answered the Hungry Thing.

''Hookies!'' cried the townspeople. ''How do you eat
them? What can they be?''

''Hookies,'' said the Wiseman, ''are known in far lands
    As a special spaghetti to eat holding hands.''

''Hookies,'' said the Cook, ''are a party dish
To serve to a guest if he isn't a fish.''

''I think,'' said the little boy, ''that it's all very simple.
Hookies . . . sound like
Lookies . . . sound like . . .

Cookies to me.''

The townspeople gave the Hungry Thing some.
And he ate them all up. Then he got to his feet.
He smiled. He patted his mouth on a line of laundry.
He turned around three times.

"Is it true
He's all through?"
Asked a lady
Dressed in blue.

"Let's all try
To say goodbye,"
Said a man
With a can.

"Come again!"
Said some men.

But the Hungry Thing just sat down again. And he pointed to his sign that said Feed Me.

"What do you want to eat?" asked the townspeople.

"Gollipops," said the Hungry Thing.

"Gollipops!" cried the townspeople. "How do you eat them? What can they be?"

"Oh, dear me!" said the Wiseman, "gollipops are new.
They are cereal shaped like toys. And sugar-coated, too!"
"Children," said the Cook, "buy them by the dozens
And trade off the box tops with classmates and cousins."

"I think," said the boy, "you all ought to hear.
Gollipops . . . sound like
Dollipops . . . sound like . . .

20

Lollipops to me."

So the townspeople gave the Hungry Thing some.

The Hungry Thing ate them all up. And he pointed to his sign again.

"Oh, please!" said the people.

"We've been here all day.

Isn't there a quicker way?"

"I think," said the boy, "that there is."

"Have some noodles?" the little boy asked the Hungry Thing. The Hungry Thing shook his head.

"Oh, excuse me. I meant to say . . . foodles."
The Hungry Thing smiled and ate them all up.

"Just look!"
Said the Cook.

"Let's all try!"
Was the cry.

So they all got busy.

"Have some smello."
They gave him some Jello.

"Have some thread."
They gave him some bread.

"Have a fanana."
They gave him a banana.

The Hungry Thing ate and ate. He looked very full.
"Is there anything more we can give you?" the townspeople wanted to know.

The Hungry Thing politely covered a hiccup.
He thought for a while. Then . . .
"Boop with a smacker," he said.

"Boop with a smacker? Boop with a smacker?
What is that?" the townspeople asked.

The boy whispered to the Wiseman. The Wiseman
whispered to the Cook. And the Cook gave the
Hungry Thing . . .

Soup with a cracker.

    The Hungry Thing ate them all up. He smiled.

He got to his feet. He wiped his mouth on the Cook's hat.

Just as he left he turned his sign around.

In big letters it said, THANK YOU!

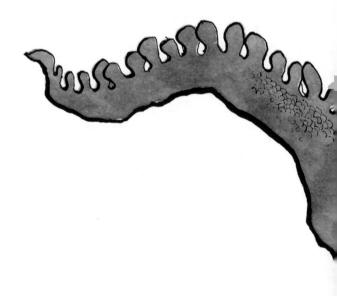